ISBN 1 85854 468 8
© Brimax Books Ltd 1996. All rights reserved.
Published by Brimax Books Ltd, Newmarket,
CB8 7AU, England 1996.
Printed in China.

Where is Giraffe?

by Lucy Kincaid
Illustrated by Peter Rutherford

BRIMAX • NEWMARKET • ENGLAND

trees

Some trees are tall.

Giraffe

All giraffes are tall.

Zebra

"Where is Giraffe?" asks Zebra.

Snake

"Where is Giraffe?" asks Snake.

Chameleon

"Where is Giraffe?" asks Chameleon.

Rhinoceros

"Where is Giraffe?" asks Rhinoceros.

Parrot

"Giraffe is here," says Parrot.

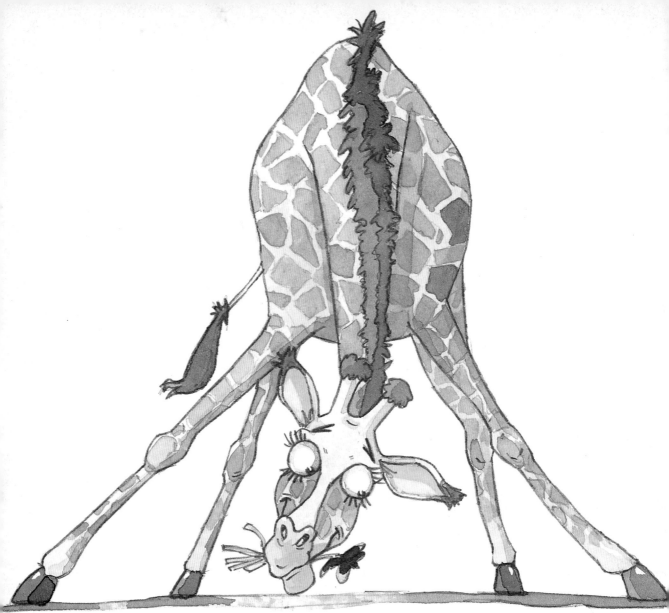

Giraffe bends down.

"I have been here all the time,"
says Giraffe.